First published in the United Kingdom in 2012 by
Portico Books
10 Southcombe Street
London
W14 0RA

An imprint of Anova Books Company Ltd

ISBN 9781907554575

A CIP catalogue record for this book is available from the
British Library.

10 9 8 7 6 5 4 3 2 1

Printed and bound by Everbest Printing, China

This book can be ordered direct from the publisher at
www.anovabooks.com

MIKE HASKINS

WHEN IN ROME...

AN ALTERNATIVE GUIDE FOR WORLD TRAVELLERS

Illustrated by Willie Ryan

PORTICO

CONTENTS

'TO TRAVEL IS TO DISCOVER
THAT EVERYONE IS WRONG
ABOUT OTHER COUNTRIES.'

ALDOUS HUXLEY

INTRODUCTION

When in Rome, the saying goes, you should do as the Romans do.

Don't get confused by this advice though. Don't turn up at Leonardo da Vinci Airport dressed in a toga, chewing some grapes and asking for directions to the nearest orgy.

You should, however, always be careful to avoid cultural mis-understandings in foreign places. But why should any problems arise? People are the same the world over. Everyone likes to be treated with a bit of politeness and respect. No one likes to have abuse poured down on them or to have unpleasant things shoved in their faces (unless they have specifically requested or paid for such services).

And yet from country to country opportunities for culture shock abound. Words, gestures and types of behaviour that are perfectly innocent in one part of the world will elsewhere land you in trouble, in a fight or maybe even in prison.

A thumbs-up to one man says 'up yours' to another; the hand extended in friendship in one country is in another the hand that is exclusively reserved for bottom wiping, and one man's cheery 'A-OK', is another's impression of an anal sphincter. And from these tiny acorns of cultural misunderstanding sprout all the troubles of the world.

But do not despair. Help is at hand. This useful guide will tell you how to avoid the worst *faux pas* when trotting the globe. It will tell you what bizarre practices you may find and what bizarre practices you may be doing without knowing it. It will tell you what to watch out for, what not to do, what not to wear and what not to leave uncovered.

Or, if you want to look at it another way, it's a handy guide on *how* to wind people up in different countries around the world.

After all, you could always take the attitude, 'When in Rome ... why not be bloody awkward and do as the Belgians do!'.

AFGHANISTAN

☻ Beware the curse of 39 ☻

Afghanistan – one of the most popular destinations in the world … for the armies of other countries.

Never let it be said that Afghans are plagued by groundless old superstitions. No, they keep coming up with brand-new ones. Recently they have developed a dramatic aversion to the number 39. And nobody is entirely sure why.

Some say the number became associated with prostitution because it featured in the number plate of a car belonging to an Afghan pimp. Now the curse has been taken to apply to all cars with registrations featuring 39.

Owners of such vehicles are subject to ridicule and/or sexual propositions. Many have felt the need to re-register their cars (for a small fee) or (for a slightly smaller fee) to get a man with a pot of paint to change their '39' into a '38'.

So beware of referring to the number 39 while in Afghanistan. Do not be seen reading John Buchan's The 39 Steps, do not order 'number 39' from a takeaway and avoid wearing that brightly coloured tin badge that came with your birthday card which says 'I am 39!'

Or in fact, thinking about it, generally just beware when travelling through Afghanistan.

¡DON'T FORGET!

Because of war and unrest Afghanistan is a very dangerous destination for the international traveller. On the plus side this means there should be plenty of package deals available at very competitive prices.

PHRASES TO REMEMBER

'Hello.' *(Salaam.)*
'Where's the toilet?' *(Dashtshuee kojast?)*
'Please say that again.' *(Khahesh mikonam dobare tekrar konid.)*

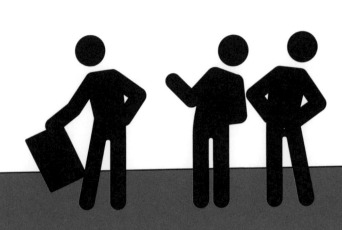

ARGENTINA

✪ Don't slap the inside of your thigh ✪

Arj'n'Tina – weren't they the names of that nice couple from the Midlands who you met on holiday last year?

No, Argentina is of course the second largest country in South America, the joint second best national football team in South America and (at last, cause for national celebration) the largest Spanish-speaking country in the world. Ha! In your face, Brazil! Serves you right for speaking Portuguese!

There are numerous ways to cause offence in Argentina just by simply pouring a glass of wine. The following methods will be taken as Argentinean insults: pouring using the left hand; pouring while holding the neck of the bottle; pouring backwards into a glass; and pouring straight over the top of your companion's head while discussing the presence of Maradona's fingerprints on certain footballs.

Another thing to avoid in Argentina is slapping the inside of the thigh near the groin. This is considered an obscene gesture. In fact, it's probably not considered a polite gesture anywhere in the world.

A danger also exists that, if this gesture goes slightly awry, you may seriously injure yourself.

So, if you end up bent over in agony after accidentally slapping your own genitals, you only have yourself to blame.

¡DON'T FORGET!

Since the Falklands/Malvinas conflict, any references to Mrs Thatcher will not go down well. And that's just in Britain.

> ### PHRASES TO REMEMBER
> 'Hello.' (*¡Hola!*)
> 'You have insulted me by pouring my wine backwards.' (*Me has insultado vertiendo mi vino al revés.*)
> 'Ow! I have just slapped myself in the testicles.' (*Ay! Acabo de darme una palmada en los testículos.*)

AUSTRALIA

Australia. Discovered in 1606 by Dutchman Willem Janszoon, then again in 1688 by William Dampier, yet again in 1770 by Captain Cook, but mostly by the native Australians from about 46,000 BC onwards.

One urban legend states, that if you turn your glass upside down in an Australian pub and place it on the bar, you are claiming to be able to fight anyone else present.

This 'tradition' is unknown to most Australians. However, now that the idea is in circulation Australians will probably be happy to beat you senseless if you really want them to. If they seem hesitant, just add a cry of 'I'll take the lot of you on, you Aussie bastards!' as you slap your inverted glass down on the bar.

Aussies instead simply appreciate a bit of politeness, good sportsmanship and respect. One thing they particularly dislike, however, is constant references to their country having once been a penal colony. The vast majority of the population immigrated to the country of their own accord in search of decent weather to have a barbie!

So be warned – if you keep making jokes about Australians being descended from prisoners, they will keep sending the likes of Dannii Minogue over in retaliation.

¡DON'T FORGET!

Aussies are a forthright, decent people who have given the world many things: the boomerang, the didgeridoo and soap operas in which the characters don't all look permanently miserable.

PHRASES TO REMEMBER

'Hello' (*G'day, mate.*)
'Do you speak English?' (*Why can't you bastards understand me?*)
'I am English.' (*I am a pommy bastard!*)

BELGIUM

✪ Snapping your fingers is vulgar ✪

Belgium, site of Napoleon's defeat at Waterloo, the headquarters of the European Union and also home to the Belgian Strawberry Museum. Belgium also gave us the Brussels sprout and provides 80 per cent of the world's billiards players with their balls. And you thought you knew this country!

You might expect this wild crazy place to have many bizarre and eccentric customs but you would be wrong.

Snapping your fingers is, however, considered to be a vulgar gesture in Belgium. So when visiting the country you should always avoid snapping your fingers, even if you happen to be listening to a really cool piece of jazz music at the time.

If Belgians are that upset by seeing people snap their fingers, you may wonder why the opening of the Flemish version of *West Side Story* wasn't followed by rioting on the streets of Antwerp.

However, what the Belgians actually find vulgar is, of course, snapping your fingers to get the attention of a waiter. Belgians are not unusual in this and will also probably find it vulgar if you try to get a waiter's attention by standing up, dropping your pants and shouting, 'Oi! Hercule Poirot! Table Six, now!'

¡DON'T FORGET!

People used to challenge each other to name seven famous Belgians. These are, of course: Adolphe Sax, Leo Baekeland, Jean-Luc Dehaene, Gerardus Mercator, Maurice Maeterlinck, Paul van Himst and Ludo Philippaerts. Now all we need to do is find out what they're famous for.

PHRASES TO REMEMBER

'Hello.' (*Goeiendag.*)
'Do you know the way to the Strawberry Museum?'
    (*Waar is le musée de la Fraise?*)
'French fries and mayonnaise please.'
    (*Frietjes met mayonnaise, alstublieft.*)

BRAZIL

✪ Where A-OK is a bum steer ✪

Covering 3.28 million square miles, Brazil is a huge, colourful country. Whether you are interested in nuts, coffee, rainforests, enormous rivers, transsexuals or particularly thorough bikini waxes, Brazil is the place for you.

Brazilians are friendly people. Nevertheless, if you enquire about their age, financial situation or marital status they will consider this very rude particularly if you have only just been introduced.

You should remember that Brazilians speak Portuguese not Spanish. If you address them in Spanish they may find it offensive. On the plus side, they may respond by teaching you some colourful Portuguese expressions you haven't heard before.

And, most importantly, in Brazil the A-OK hand gesture does not carry the positive meaning that it has in other countries. Rather than conveying a sense of optimism and happiness, the circle formed by the finger and thumb says to a Brazilian, 'Look! I have used my finger and thumb to form an image of an anal sphincter! And that, sir, is what I think of you!'

So be particularly careful when scuba diving in Brazil. If you signal to a fellow diver that everything is OK, he will think you are calling him an arsehole.

¡DON'T FORGET!

Brazilians also regard the number 24 as being strongly associated with homosexuality. So when visiting Rio de Janeiro be aware that any loudly voiced opinions about high points in the television career of Kiefer Sutherland may be misinterpreted.

PHRASES TO REMEMBER

'Hello.' (*¡Hola!*)
'Tell me about your age, financial situation and marital status.' (*Me mande informações sobre a sua idade, situação financeira e estado civil.*)
'Why are you looking angry when everything is OK?' (*Por que você esta enraivada se esta tudo bem?*)

BRUNEI

✪ It's *extremely* rude to point ✪

Brunei is a small independent country situated on the island of Borneo. It is covered in mangrove swamps and forests with a few well-dressed people standing in between them.

Over the years the inhabitants of Brunei have benefited from the country's oil and gas reserves and pay no personal income tax or capital gains tax. The name for the inhabitants of Brunei is 'rich'. Or alternatively, 'Bruneian'.

When greeting people in Brunei the custom is to touch hands lightly and then put your hand to your chest. Try not to make this look like you have decided to wipe your hand on your shirt immediately after shaking hands.

And when pointing out a particularly interesting mangrove swamp, forest or rich-looking individual in Brunei, remember never to stick out your finger as you do so.

Pointing with the finger is considered a very impolite gesture in the tiny sultanate. Instead, fold the fingers of your right hand under your thumb and then use your thumb to point.

Using this gesture may also, of course, result in you hitchhiking by accident, possibly in the general direction of the thing at which you had been trying to point.

¡DON'T FORGET!

Brunei is an independent sultanate. It is not what Scottish people call members of the junior division of the Girl Guides.

PHRASES TO REMEMBER

'What's new?' (*Khabar Terbaru?*)
'You're very kind!' (*Anda sangat baik!*)
'What do you do for a living?' (*Apakah Pekerjaan Anda?*)

BULGARIA

✪ Shaking your head means yes ✪

It would be a dull world if there wasn't a place where the meanings of nodding and shaking the head were completely reversed. And that place is Bulgaria.

Ah, Bulgaria. You know. Beneath Romania, next to Serbia, just the other side of the Republic of Macedonia, balanced on top of Greece and Turkey on the edge of the Black Sea. Yes, that's the one!

Over the years Bulgarians have given the world many great inventions. These include the first electronic calculation machine, the digital watch and the airbag. And yet to this day Bulgarians remain in defiance of the rest of the world when it comes to the meaning of nodding and shaking the head. When a resident of Bulgaria shakes his head, this means 'yes'. And, somewhat inevitably, when a Bulgarian nods his head, this means 'no'.

According to legend, this practice developed during the country's domination by the Ottoman Empire. Bulgarians supposedly learned to reverse the meaning of shaking and nodding heads in order to confuse their Turkish occupiers. Why they persist with this ruse several centuries after the Ottoman Empire reached its height remains a mystery. It's enough to leave anyone nodding their heads.

¡DON'T FORGET!

This reversal of meanings can make the simplest conversation fraught with danger. Stand well back if an ignorant non-Bulgarian visits Sofia and receives a cheerful nod of the head in response to statements such as 'Are you looking at me?', 'Do you think I look stupid or something?' and 'Do you want to make something of it, pal?'

PHRASES TO REMEMBER

'Hello.' (*Zdravey.*)
'Yes.' (*Dah.*)
'No.' (*Ne.*)

CAMBODIA

✪ Never pat a Cambodian on the head ✪

In 1980, punk band the Dead Kennedys famously attempted to popularise the notion of a 'Holiday in Cambodia'. Today this campaign is finally beginning to pay off, with the tropical country now receiving about 2 million visitors a year.

If you do visit Cambodia, however, you should refrain from any inclination you may have to ruffle the hair of any of the local residents. No, not even very little Cambodians with particularly cute tufty heads of hair. Touching anyone on the head for any reason is considered extremely impolite.

In Cambodia, as well as in other countries in Southeast Asia, the head is regarded as the highest spiritual part of the body. It is the centre of a person's intelligence and sacred substance. And, quite reasonably, the locals will not want your greasy mitts all over the centre of their sacred substance.

Also, of course, they don't want to have their expensive hairdos messed up for the rest of the day.

So keep your hands to yourself! What kind of person are you, anyway? Travelling halfway round the world to wander through foreign cities tousling the heads of complete strangers?

¡DON'T FORGET!

The best-known people in Britain in the 1960s and 70s were perhaps The Beatles and Morecambe and Wise. In Cambodia during the same period it was Pol Pot and the Khmer Rouge. You should, however, avoid bringing up their names in conversation, as their work is no longer widely celebrated.

PHRASES TO REMEMBER!

'Hello.' (*Suor-sdei.*)
'Do you speak English?' (*Teu nak niyeay phea sar anglei tay?*)
'Where are you going?' (*Teu nak kampong toev na?*)

CANADA

❂ Don't eat on the street ❂

Canada – the more modest, more softly spoken and rather better-endowed North American country. Yes, Canada covers a slightly larger area than the USA.

OK, admittedly the population all have to cluster together for warmth in the tiny area of Canada that isn't covered in permafrost. Nevertheless, they are a famously polite people. So, if you pay them a visit, make sure you are on your best behaviour and wipe your feet when you touch down at Montréal-Pierre Elliott Trudeau International Airport.

One thing that Canadians certainly regard as bad manners is eating out on the street. So, when buying a Canadian takeaway, do not start scoffing it the moment you step out of the emporium in which you purchased it. Take it home with you, set it out on a plate at the dining table, tuck a napkin into your collar and then consume it slowly and thoughtfully.

Canadians are a clean and health-loving people. They regard stuffing fast food down yourself while wandering around town as something that is done by the vulgar people who live in the country just below them.

So do not eat on the street in Canada. You should definitely use a plate instead.

¡DON'T FORGET!

The temperature in Canada regularly drops to –40 degrees. This is quite chilly, so take an extra jumper with you and don't be tempted to eat any yellow snow.

PHRASES TO REMEMBER

'Hello.' (*Hello.*)
'Is this another of those countries where they speak English.' (*Yes it is.*)
'But you speak French as well, don't you?' (*Oui.*)

CHILE

○ Keep your fingers together ○

The modern country of Chile was founded in 1818 by the splendidly named Bernardo O'Higgins. Home of Augusto Pinochet, the world's driest desert and the world's most famous miners, Chile is also the world's longest thinnest country. Over 2,700 miles long but never more than 150 miles across, Chile must surely be regarded by other countries as a sort of geographical supermodel.

When in Chile you should avoid beckoning using your hand as this is considered impolite. Making a fist and holding it level with your head will also go down badly as it will be seen as a communist gesture, while slapping the fist into the palm of the other hand will be considered obscene.

And in Chile, holding your palm upwards and then spreading your fingers is an insulting gesture used to suggest that a person is lacking in the brain department.

So be careful when being given change in Santiago. If you spread your fingers, not only will you drop your coins but the shopkeeper may respond angrily with: 'Who are you calling stupid?'

¡DON'T FORGET!

Chilean people may seem less concerned about personal space than other nationalities. They will therefore often stand very close to you during conversation, even when you point out that their country is actually quite big.

PHRASES TO REMEMBER

'Hello.' (*¡Hola!*)
'Come here!' (*Ven aquí!*)
'Why are you standing so close to me?'
    (*¿Por qué te estás quedando tan cerca de mí?*)

CHINA

☼ Never give a clock as a gift ☼

The Mysterious Orient. The Land of Eastern Promise. The Chinese Empire. These are just a few names of takeaway restaurants founded by people of Chinese descent.

China itself is famous for having more cultural taboos than you can shake a chopstick at. In fact, shaking a chopstick is itself considered the height of bad manners in China. Well, it is if you're shaking it to make noise or draw attention to yourself.

Another way to cause offence in China is to give a timepiece as a gift. A clock or watch is not regarded as a glamorous or useful gift. Instead, it is the gift that tells the lucky recipient he or she is going to die. This fact is unlikely to be used by the Chinese watch and clock industry as a catchy advertising slogan.

But why this hang-up? Firstly, Chinese people regard a clock as a present which the recipient can watch as it counts down the seconds towards his or her death. Secondly, the phrase 'to gift a clock' in Mandarin sounds the same as the word 'terminating' or 'attending a funeral'.

So bear that in mind on the day they hand you a clock at your retirement party from work!

¡DON'T FORGET!

Chopsticks should never be left standing upright in a bowl of rice or other food. The sticks will then resemble the incense sticks standing on an altar at a funeral service. Besides, if you place your chopsticks upright in your food, you could sneeze or unexpectedly lean forward and end up with a chopstick lodged up each nostril.

PHRASES TO REMEMBER

'Hello.' (*Ni hao.*)
'What time is it?' (*Xian zai ji dian?*)
'Could you take my picture please?' (*Qing gei wo pai yi xia?*)

COLOMBIA

✪ Mind your elbows ✪

Named after Christopher Columbus, Colombia spans the top of South America from the Pacific to the Caribbean. The country has given the world Nobel Prize-winning author Gabriel Garcia Marquez, pop singer Shakira and 12 per cent of the world's coffee.

There are a number of things to avoid when visiting Colombia. Adult men should not wear shorts (although they should definitely wear some form of trousers) and women should not wear open sandals.

Colombians are understandably not keen to discuss the massive illegal trade in class A drugs. This is therefore not a good subject for polite conversation and you will not find any of these substances for sale in the Duty Free area of Bogota Airport.

Colombians also consider it rude if you tap the underside of your elbow with the fingers of your other hand. If you make this gesture to a Colombian you are telling them that you think they are stingy.

If, however, you manage to tap the underside of your elbow with the fingers of the same hand, this will amaze Colombians and everyone else. It will mean you are either the world's greatest contortionist or you have just suffered a particularly unpleasant arm injury.

¡DON'T FORGET!

If Colombian customs officers search your bags and discover your container of Johnson's baby powder has emptied all over your suitcase, you are probably going to miss your flight home.

PHRASES TO REMEMBER

'Hello.' (¡Hola!))
'My elbow is itchy.' (Me pica el codo.)
'I promise you it is talcum powder.' (Te prometo que es talco.)

CYPRUS

✪ Don't put toilet paper down the toilet ✪

The Mediterranean island of Cyprus has been inhabited by man for at least 10,000 years and thus has many long-established traditions. One that is most notable to visiting tourists is that pertaining to the disposal of toilet paper.

When visiting Cyprus your used toilet paper should not be disposed of in the lavatory bowl. Instead, you are told to place used sheets in the bin. Hopefully a small bin will be provided for this purpose so you will not have to waddle out to the bins at the back of your hotel with your pants round your ankles.

Although clear instructions are given, many travellers find themselves psychologically unable to place the reams of soiled paper that they have produced in the bin provided. Instead, they check around for CCTV equipment before surreptitiously dropping their paper in the toilet bowl and creeping away like lavatorial terrorists.

These people are willing to risk blocking the Cypriot sewage system rather than put their toilet paper in a bin. They would clearly prefer to be sought out by the authorities and perhaps paraded on the evening news bulletin as the person responsible for causing the entire island's effluence network to explode.

¡DON'T FORGET!

Other possible options for the disposal of toilet paper also exist but again are not recommended. Throwing used sheets out of an adjacent window is likely to cause offence to local residents, while putting it in your suitcase to take home with you will not go down well if you have your bags searched by customs.

PHRASES TO REMEMBER

'Hello.' (*Yassou.*)
'Where is the toilet, please?' (*Pou ine i touale'tes?*)
'Stop, stop, help!' (*Stamatiste! Stamatiste! Voithia!*)

EGYPT

✪ Tapping your fingers is an indecent proposal ✪

Egypt – home of the pharaohs, the pyramids and that funny little red hat that Tommy Cooper used to wear.

Egypt first became a unified country over 5,000 years ago. This has given its inhabitants time to build up an impressive range of cultural taboos ready to catch out the unwary traveller.

As in other Arab countries, pointing is seen as rude, while the left hand is regarded as the unclean hand which should not be used to shake hands or for eating. If you point using your left hand, you will presumably be immediately deported.

When shaking hands in Egypt, follow up the shake with a touch on the elbow. Do not, however, touch the elbow with your unclean left hand or the other person will look displeased and will stand trying to sniff their elbow.

And tapping your index fingers together side by side has a surprisingly sexually suggestive meaning. In Egypt bashing the edges of the first fingers of each hand together is a gesture used to suggest sexual congress.

You thought you were just comparing the lengths of your two index fingers but what you were in fact saying was: 'Hello! Who fancies a quick one?'

¡DON'T FORGET!

The Great Pyramids of Egypt are still standing after 4,500 years. So be careful if you go near them. You don't want to go down in history as the person who dislodged the stone that was holding them all up.

PHRASES TO REMEMBER

'Hello.' (*Ahlan wa sahlan.*)
'May I have the bill please?' (*Mumkin el-Hisab, min fadlak?*)
'I Love Egypt!' (*Ana Baheb Masr!*)

ETHIOPIA

Who doesn't like a nice cup of coffee at the end of dinner? Mormons, people who have to get up early the next morning, people with an allergy that causes them to vomit prodigiously for several hours after drinking coffee, people who prefer tea … OK, lots of people. Ethiopians, however, *love* a cup of coffee.

The remains of the earliest-known ancestors of modern humans dating from 5.5 million years ago have been found in Ethiopia. And archaeologists are agreed on one thing. After 5.5 million years, the Ethiopians must surely know a thing or two about serving coffee.

You should never refuse an invitation to an Ethiopian coffee drinking ritual. Guests sit on the floor while frankincense burns in the background. Coffee beans are washed before them, roasted over charcoal, ground, mixed with sugar and water and their aroma inhaled. The coffee is then served first to the eldest person present. This would presumably be the Ethiopian equivalent of Gareth Hunt in the old Nescafé adverts.

The pot or jebena is then filled and refilled for first, second and third servings known as the awol, the tona and finally the baraka, which is also called the 'this-coffee's-beginning-to-get-a-bit-weak-now' round.

¡DON'T FORGET!

The predominant climate in Ethiopia is tropical monsoon. So you're going to look a bit silly if you turn up not having packed an umbrella because you thought it never rained.

PHRASES TO REMEMBER

*'Hello.' (*Hello.*)
'Coffee please.' (*You don't have any Nescafé Gold Blend, do you?*)
'Thank you.' (*Ta.*)
English is the official language of Ethopia.

FIJI

✪ A Fijian handshake can last the *entire* conversation ✪

Fiji – its status as a tropical paradise was once slightly sullied by its reputation for cannibalism. But, luckily, no longer! The last person to suffer this fate was the Reverend Thomas Baker in 1867. Baker had attempted to retrieve something from the head of a Fijian village chief. His boot (complete with teeth marks) is today on display in the local museum. It is therefore advisable to avoid attempting to retrieve anything from the heads of local chiefs.

Today Fijians are much friendlier. Shaking hands was introduced to the island in the 19th century and Fijians have taken to the practice like nobody's business. A Fijian may not stop shaking hands with you for the entire duration of your conversation.

So, when visiting the area, prepare to have your hand left reeling after even the briefest of meetings. Alternatively, if you suffer from poor circulation in your fingers you will surely be cured by a visit to this Pacific archipelago, and the blood will be left surging around your hand at high speed.

Goodness knows what it's like in Fiji on New Year's Eve. If they take your hands to sing 'Auld Lang Syne', you could be there until midsummer.

¡DON'T FORGET!

Cannibalism has been off the menu in Fiji for nearly 150 years. If you visit it is probably best to avoid mentioning the practice or indeed making any attempts to revive it.

> ## PHRASES TO REMEMBER
>
> 'Knock down the price.' (*Dam thora kamti karo.*)
> 'Lower it more.' (*Aur kamti.*)
> 'Just looking.' (*Khali dekhta.*)

FRANCE

⊙ Discussing jobs and money is taboo ⊙

The concept of the faux pas must surely have originated in France. Why else would it have a French name? This is surely the reason why the French constantly look so sniffy about everything. They have to put up with the rest of us faux pas-ing around from lundi to dimanche every week.

Surprisingly, things which do not seem to count as faux pas in France include body odour, luxuriant underarm hair on women and persistent surliness. Nevertheless, the French are renowned for their culture, elegance, style and several hundred varieties of cheese.

The French do, however, have a range of social non-nons that the visitor to the country should avoid. Of these, the discussion of money is said to be their greatest taboo. The French do not like to show off their wealth. Displays of expensive clothes, status symbols and jewellery are frowned upon. This may be one reason why France has not made a significant contribution to the world of hip-hop.

So, if you are invited for a meal in France, do not rattle your jewellery, boast about your expensive possessions or bring along a slideshow of your bank statements to show by way of after-dinner entertainment.

¡DON'T FORGET!

Belching is considered to be extremely ill-mannered in France. French people would prefer you to fart than to belch. Many believe this is the main cultural difference between the French and the British.

PHRASES TO REMEMBER

'Hello.' (*Salut.*)
'How much do you earn?' (*Combien gagnes-tu?*)
'Do you mind if I fart?' (*Ça t'embête si je pète?*)

GERMANY

✪ Never shake hands with one hand in your pocket ✪

Germany's reputation and popularity has varied somewhat over the years. These days, Germany is an economic powerhouse at the heart of Europe. Its people are successful, affluent and frequently naked whether you want them to be or not. They are renowned for the speed at which they can claim a sun-lounger, their chant of 'no world wars but three world cups!' and for being the only country in Europe to have any money left.

You should therefore be careful to observe correct etiquette when dealing with German business colleagues. A German will find it rude if you keep one hand in your pocket while offering the other to him to shake. So, when greeting a German, allow him to see what you're doing with both your hands.

Germans will also consider it rude if you keep both hands in your pockets while attempting to shake hands.

The handshaking problem will obviously not arise if you and your German friend are shaking hands on the beach and both happen to be stark naked at the time. In this instance, you should still be aware that the opportunity for offence may arise as a result of the position of your other hand.

¡DON'T FORGET!

Rather understandably, modern Germans do not enjoy being constantly reminded about the war by British people who still seem obsessed with the subject. So do not conclude that Germans 'have no sense of humour' just because they don't join in with your impressions and silly walk!

PHRASES TO REMEMBER

'Hello.' (*Gutentag.*)
'It is good to be naked.' (*Nackt sein ist eine gute sache.*)
'Help! My hand is stuck in my pocket!' (*Hilfe! Meine hand ist in meiner hosentasche stecken geblieben!*)

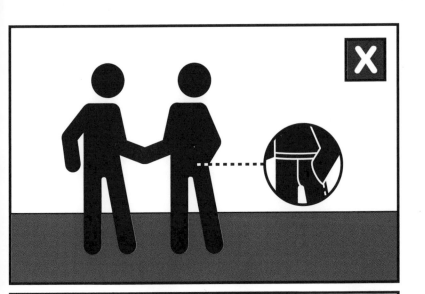

GHANA

☻ Don't beckon people with a raised palm ☻

There are various methods of beckoning people towards you. In different cultures, some of these will be regarded as impolite if not downright insulting. Summoning people with a wave of the hand or fingers is generally considered better manners than doing the same using the genitals or buttocks. Nevertheless, certain beckoning gestures using the hand may still cause offence.

When visiting Ghana never call anyone over by twitching one or more fingers while your palm is facing upwards. To Ghanaians this gesture does not mean 'Please would you come here'. Instead, it has the slightly less polite meaning of 'I believe you to be a prostitute'.

You should particularly bear this in mind if you get a job directing traffic in the middle of Ghana's capital city Accra. Waving vehicles on with your palm raised will quickly cause a build-up of several hundred gridlocked drivers around you, every one of whom you have just accused of being a sex worker.

The summoning gesture that is preferred in Ghana is performed with the palm facing downwards and the fingers waving towards the self. If, however, you repeat this gesture in other countries, people may presume you have a limp wrist.

¡DON'T FORGET!

Ghana was once a British colony known as the Gold Coast but disappointingly a lot of the coast is in fact sand.

PHRASES TO REMEMBER

*'Hello.' (*Do I stick out like a sore thumb?*)
'I'm looking for a good time?' (*Take me to where the locals go.*)
'Why do all these drivers look so angry?' (*Get me out of here!*)
*English is the official language of Ghana.

GREECE

✪ Be careful how you wave ✪

Greece – the country that gave the world Plato, Sophocles, Aristotle, Pythagoras, Archimedes, Homer, the original Olympic Games and, more recently, Nana Mouskouri and Demis Roussos. Yes, Greece, as they say, is the word.

These days, Greece is slightly short of cash. This has led to some expressions of public disgust towards the authorities. One long-established method of expressing disgust in Greek is the 'moutza'.

The moutza is made by holding the palm upright with the fingers outstretched and is a well-known and terrible insult. The moutza refers to an ancient Byzantine practice when chained prisoners would be led through a village so the locals could punish them. This punishment was performed using the cheapest, most readily available, least pleasant material to hand. Yes, the unfortunate prisoners quite literally had faeces shoved in their faces.

So if you really want to get your point across and maybe get beaten up in the process, thrust your palm into a Greek person's face while saying 'na!' or 'here you go!'

In short, this is the way to tell a Greek person to consume a dollop of something that is of similar consistency but considerably less pleasant-tasting than hummus.

¡DON'T FORGET!

Because of the moutza gesture you should be very careful when trying to order five of anything in a Greek shop.

PHRASES TO REMEMBER

'Hello.' (*Yassou.*)
'A table for two please.' (*Ena trapezi ya thio atoma, parakalo.*)
'I'd like to hire a boat.' (*Tha eethela na neekyaso meea parka.*)

HONG KONG

✪ Try not to be such a winker ✪

Hong Kong of course has cultural taboos aplenty. Be careful where you aim the spout of your teapot while you are there. Pointing it at an individual means you are challenging them to a fight. Apples are not a good present for people in hospital as 'apple' in the Shanghai dialect sounds like 'death from disease'.

And green hats are rarely seen in Hong Kong because in Chinese culture they signify infidelity. So some confusion must surely arise each year when the local expats celebrate St Patrick's Day.

You may also think that if you wink at a resident of Hong Kong they will regard you as a cheery, friendly, cheeky chappy. You would be wrong. They will regard you as a disgusting sex pest. The people of Hong Kong, as in China and India, regard winking as being extremely rude. In Hong Kong, winking may be taken as an insult or a sexual proposition.

The act of winking thus conveys a look of disdain and contempt combined with a disgusting sexual come-on. And indeed many have long suspected that this is exactly what Anne Robinson is trying to convey at the end of each episode of *The Weakest Link*.

¡DON'T FORGET!

It is against the law to drop any litter in Hong Kong. If you even drop your keys you will be liable to a large fine. So you could simultaneously be thousands of Hong Kong dollars out of pocket and unable to get back into your apartment.

PHRASES TO REMEMBER!

'Hello.' (*Nehih ho ma?*)
'Yummy, very delicious.' (*Ho ho sik.*)
'Does anyone speak English?' (*Yáuhmóuh yàhn sik góng yìngmán a?*)

HUNGARY

Founded in 896, Hungary is one of the oldest countries in Europe, pre-dating France and Germany. When sharing a drink with a Hungarian to congratulate him on this achievement, you should, however, avoid clinking glasses to say cheers.

At the sound of the clink your Hungarian friend will become suddenly upset. He will thump down his glass and demand to know why you are insulting the 13 Martyrs of Arad.

The tale of the 13 Martyrs is indeed chilling. Following suppression of the Hungarian Revolution of 1848–49, the country was brought back under Hapsburg rule. The leaders of the revolution were summarily executed. The Austrian generals who carried out the executions were believed to have grimly mixed business with pleasure by downing mugs of beer which they clinked together in celebration of the Hungarian defeat.

The people of Hungary thus vowed not to clink their beer glasses for 150 years after the executions. Theoretically, this moratorium on glass clinking ended in 1999. Nevertheless, many Hungarians still consider a cheery clink to be in poor taste. So don't try this in a Hungarian bar or you may end up with a roomful of Magyars emptying their beer over your head.

¡DON'T FORGET!

Among many great Hungarian inventors are Laszlo Biro and Erno Rubik, one of whom invented the biro pen and the other the Rubik cube, although it is very difficult to remember which invented which. Another Hungarian gift to the world was the noiseless match invented by Janos Irinyi (who presumably made no noise when you struck him).

PHRASES TO REMEMBER

'Hello.' (*Sziasztok*)
'A beer please.' (*Egy sort kerek.*)
'Cheers!' (*Egészségedre!*)

INDIA

⊘ What does the Indian head wobble mean? ⊘

The Indian head wobble. You must have seen it. The Indian head in question seems to simultaneously shake, nod and generally shimmy around on top of the Indian neck while its Indian owner patiently listens to what someone is telling him.

It is a very pleasing and relaxing gesture to watch. You should look away occasionally though in case you begin to feel seasick. The head wobble is nevertheless the most impressively Indian spectacle you will ever witness.

But what exactly does the head wobble mean? Many ignorant people have suggested explanations for the gesture. These include the suggestion that a high proportion of Indian people once worked in the road-drilling business, thereby damaging their cervicobrachial regions, or that they have spent too long watching a nodding dog toy in the back of someone's car. These are ridiculous and very stupid explanations and should never be repeated under any circumstances.

The head wobble is in fact a non-verbal equivalent to the Hindi word aacha. Aacha has many meanings ranging from 'good' to 'I understand'.

OK. Got that? Just wobble your head if you understand.

¡DON'T FORGET!

The cow is a sacred animal in India. So try to avoid wandering around the country dressed from head to foot in your leather bondage gear.

PHRASES TO REMEMBER

'Hello.' (*Namasté.*)
'I don't understand what you are saying.' (*Meri samajh mei nahin aaya.*)
'Do you want to go home? (*Kya, aap ghar jaanaa chahte hain?*)

INDONESIA

✪ Don't eat everything on your plate ✪

When you were a child you were always being told not to waste your food, you had to eat everything on your plate before getting your pudding and if you licked your plate clean this would save mummy from having to do any washing up.

In Indonesia, however, it is customary to always leave a little food uneaten. Do not worry about this! This small portion of uneaten food will not be served up to you again and again at subsequent mealtimes until you finally eat it.

Instead, leaving a small part of your food will be taken as a sign that you have been fully satisfied. If you empty your plate, this will say to your Indonesian hosts, 'You call that a dinner! I'm still starving! I'm probably going to have to pick up a takeaway on my way home!'

An empty plate in Indonesia means that you would like more food. It will then be piled up with more nosh which you will feel obliged to keep eating until you are a similar size to Mount Semeru in East Java.

So clear your plate at your peril if you ever want to leave the dinner table.

¡DON'T FORGET!

Indonesia literally means 'Indian archipelago'. The country comprises thousands of different islands. So don't worry. It was like that when you got there. You didn't break it.

> ## PHRASES TO REMEMBER
> 'Hello.' (*Halo.*)
> 'I'm hungry' (*Saya lapar.*)
> 'I really like it!' (*Saya suka sekali!*)

IRAN

✪ Thumbs down to the thumbs up ✪

Over the last few decades it would be putting it mildly to say that oil-rich Iran has had a few 'issues' with other developed countries' greedy foreign policies and sneaky democratic ideals. And maybe it's their distrust of lies, greed and the good ol' U. S. of A. that has seen them come to dislike the vulgar Western gesture of the 'thumbs up'?

To an Iranian, the thumbs up is not a cheerful sign of a generally positive and optimistic outlook. Instead, the gesture means something similar to sticking up your second finger. The thumbs up thus represents something obscene. It says 'swivel on this', 'up yours' and/or 'screw you'.

This is possibly the reason why Paul 'Thumbs Up Macca' McCartney has never been asked to perform there.

An Iranian will therefore take your thumbs-up gesture as you telling him where you would like him to stick his carpet, his big beard, his atomic weapons programme or whatever else he is currently showing off to you.

Wouldn't it be ironic if sticking up a single middle digit was a positive friendly sign in Iran?

¡DON'T FORGET!

If you spot an Iranian, or are lucky enough to meet one in person (as opposed to just on *News at Ten*), instead of giving them a thumbs up, shake their hand firmly, look them in the eye and apologise profusely for the imminent Coalition invasion of their country.

> ### PHRASES TO REMEMBER!
> 'Hello.' (*Salam.*)
> 'Make yourself at home!' (*Inja khaneh shomast!*)
> 'I'm just kidding.' (*Shookhi mikonam.*)

IRAQ

✪ Mind you don't put your foot in it ✪

In 2003, Saddam Hussein's statue in Baghdad was toppled and some Iraqis immediately began walloping the effigy with their shoes. In December 2008, during a news conference in the city, President Bush narrowly missed being hit in the face by two well-aimed brogues. The message must be clear (even to President Bush). Watch out for low-flying shoes in Baghdad.

And not only that, showing the soles of the shoe or foot is the most terrible insult in Arabic culture. And being whacked straight in the mush by someone's size-11 boot is possibly even worse.

Yes, in the Arab world the feet are regarded as an unclean part of the body. You should therefore avoid touching anyone with your feet, sitting with your feet up pointing at someone or just raising your feet in anyone's direction. Not only will this be insulting to the other person, you are also likely to tip over backwards.

The offensiveness of the sole of the foot is not, however, unique to Arabic society. If you wake up after a night on the town with someone's footprint on your face, this was probably not left there by someone being polite or friendly.

¡DON'T FORGET!

In Arabic culture, as well as the feet being unclean, the left hand is similarly tainted as it is reserved for 'bodily hygiene'. This does not mean that you should attempt to use your feet for 'bodily hygiene'. If you attempt to wipe your bottom using your feet you will do yourself an injury or topple over and fall in the toilet.

PHRASES TO REMEMBER

'Hello.' (*Marhaban.*)
'I need help, please.' (*Ahtajoo ilal musa'ada raja'an*)
'Great!' (*Azeem!*)

ISRAEL

✪ Don't point a finger in the open palm of the other hand ✪

When it comes to its place in the world, Israel can confidently lay claim to more self-esteem issues than any other place on Earth, except perhaps Greece which is currently also going through a bad patch. Israelites, you would think, have enough on their plate without worrying about the little things that unruly travellers would get up too upon arrival into their beautiful land, but like most developed countries with a democracy, polite customs and etiquettes prevail no matter how ridiculous they appear to the outside world. But seeing as Israel is actually separated off from the outside world by a gigantic barrier, we'll let them off.

Upon arriving into Ben Gurion Airport, you would be quick to learn that pointing your middle finger in the open palm of your other hand, as if almost gesturing to do a 'time out' is a social no-no. This offensive piece of physical theatre, or insult as they are more commonly known, basically implies that whoever the motion is aimed at is full of crap. It's sort of the physical representation of that popular Western phrase 'whatever'. Which never gets old, does it?

¡DON'T FORGET!

With a population almost the size of London, in a state eight times *smaller* than US sunshine state Florida, Israel has lot of people, in an enclosed area remember, that you should try and not piss off.

> ## PHRASES TO REMEMBER
>
> 'Hello.' (*Shalom.*)
> 'Is everything OK?' (*Hakol Beseder?*)
> 'A cup of tea, please.' (*Cos tay, bevakasha.*)

ITALY

✪ Careful with your devil horns ✪

Form a fist. Hold down the second and third fingers with your thumb and raise the index and little fingers. Now hold your hand aloft for all to see! Rock and roll! It's the gesture popularised by heavy metal singer Ronnie James Dio.

In Italy, Spain and South America, however, the gesture has a different meaning. In these regions, the use of the horns gesture may not convey enthusiasm for excruciating guitar solos and long-haired men in spandex. Instead, it is the symbol of the cuckolded husband and will say to an Italian, 'Buongiorno, signore. I hear your lovely wife is a bit of a slapper.' This is unlikely to go down well in Italy, Spain or indeed anywhere.

In Italy, the symbol is also used to ward off the devil or the evil eye. Meanwhile, at the University of Texas, the same symbol yet again is used to show support for the college football team.

One hand gesture, three meanings. Maybe if you make the gesture at an Italian he will take it as meaning, 'Your wife has been possessed by Satan and is currently being unfaithful to you with the University of Texas college football team.'

¡DON'T FORGET!

Famous Italians include Marco Polo, Christopher Columbus, Sebastian Cabot and the Mafia. So, if you annoy an Italian, they will be able to hunt you down no matter where you hide in the world.

PHRASES TO REMEMBER

'Hello.' (*Ciao.*)
'Your wife looks a friendly woman.' (*La tua moglie sembra una donna amichevole.*)
'What is this horse's head doing in my bed?' (*Che sta facendo questa testa di cavallo nel mio letto?*)

JAPAN

✪ Putting a brave face on it ✪

A broad smile plastered across someone's face may tell you many things. It can tell you that the person is feeling happy. It can tell you that they are feeling optimistic. It can tell you that they want to make a good impression. Or it can tell you that they were just watching a moment earlier when you fell flat on your face after slipping in a dog turd.

In Japan, however, a smile may not indicate that a person is happy. The Japanese may smile instead to denote confusion, embarrassment or sadness. Confused? Well, this all goes back a few years. In olden times, it was considered a breach of their code of honour if Samurai women looked sorrowful upon learning that their men had died in battle. Instead, the ladies had to grin from ear to ear on hearing the news. It must have looked like they were about to receive a significant insurance payment.

So remember, a cheerful-looking Japanese person may not be happy. They may have just learned that a loved one has recently suffered a terrible accident involving a scimitar.

¡DON'T FORGET!

When entering someone's house in Japan, you should always remove your shoes. Do not get confused and remove everything *except* your shoes.

> ### PHRASES TO REMEMBER
>
> 'Hello.' (*Konnichiwa.*)
> 'Could you take my picture, please?' (*Shasin wo totte morae masu ka?*)
> 'I'm not an American.' (*Watashi wa amerika-jin dewa arimasen.*)

LEBANON

❂ Best to leave your eyebrows alone ❂

Lebanon, former homeland of the Phoenicians, who created one of the world's first-known written alphabets. So the Lebanese gave us the written word (sort of). And, as most people will agree, this has proved to be ever so handy over the years!

The ancient Phoenician city of Byblos is the oldest continually occupied city in the world. As the centre of the papyrus trade, the name of the city of Byblos was even adapted as the name of quite a famous book. Can you guess which one?

Today in Lebanon, one gesture you should be careful of is fiddling with your eyebrows in public. Licking your little finger and brushing it across your eyebrow tells someone that you believe them to be a homosexual.

So when in Lebanon do your eyebrow grooming in private! Or at least do it at a safe distance from anyone who might take offence at being called a homosexual. And you may find quite a few such people in Lebanon.

Generally, just avoid playing with your eyebrows near anyone likely to be upset when your discarded eyebrow hairs descend over them in the warm Beirut air like a swarm of hideous insects.

¡DON'T FORGET!

Lebanon borders Israel and Syria. So when visiting Lebanon try to avoid asking the inhabitants if they ever have any problems with their neighbours.

PHRASES TO REMEMBER

'Hello.' (*Marhvaba.*)
'Tell us a joke.' (*Khabbrouna shi nekteh?*)
'What's up dude?' (*Shu ya hobb?*)

MEXICO

✪ Don't place hands on hips. It's a sign of hostility ✪

Ah, Mexicans. They gave the world chocolate, tomatoes and the number '0'. Actually, that was the Mayans. But 'what's the difference?' I hear you say. Adored throughout the world, the beautiful Spanish language gave drugs a cool surname – Cartel, and their government is a well-established group of tennis-fanatics, constantly associated with the terms 'backhanders' and 'racketeering'.

In many places around the world, putting your hands on your hips is seen as a sign of nothing exciting except, perhaps, overt friendliness or frustration at having to wait for hours in a pointless queue at the post office.

In Mexico, it means the exact opposite: hands placed on the hips invites a physical challenge, a fight, a scuffle. To a Mexican, this action is the verbal equivalent of 'Come and have a go if you think you're hard enough' or, in Spanish, '*Venga y disfrute de una oportunidad si crees que eres lo suficientemente fuerte*' which, actually, kind of sounds quite romantic and alluring. But don't be fooled – they're out for blood.

¡DON'T FORGET!

Mexicans speak Spanish, but Mexico is *not* in Spain. Don't make that mistake. In fact, the two places are oceans apart. Literally.

PHRASES TO REMEMBER

'Welcome.' (*Bienvenida.*)
'How are you?' (*Cómo esta?*)
'Your country is much better at football than mine!'
    (*Tu estas país está mejor que el mío en el fútbol!*)

MONGOLIA

✪ Watch what you're doing with that yurt ✪

Mongolia is one of the world's most remote places. Unless, of course, you live there, in which case it couldn't be less remote.

Mongolian herdsmen are known for their hospitality. Nevertheless many taboos surround their yurts. It is offensive to step on the threshold of the yurt as this may annoy a malicious spirit. Furthermore you should not enter the yurt with a horsewhip in your hand. So leave your horsewhip on the right side of the yurt door and generally try and overcome your desire to whip horses inside somebody's home.

Mongolians consider water to be a deity. So if you strip off to give yourself a good scrub in a Mongolian river this is likely to offend as well as to cause parts of your body to turn blue and snap off in the cold.

Also in Mongolia it is considered shameful to urinate towards the setting or rising sun. Urinating shows disrespect to the sun which warms and illuminates the world. Similarly, in Britain it is disrespectful if you urinate towards a representative of your electricity supply company as he walks up your garden path to read your meter.

¡DON'T FORGET!

Even though Mongolia is divided into Inner Mongolia and Outer Mongolia, this does not mean that Inner Mongolia is inside and under cover. So remember to take a coat.

PHRASES TO REMEMBER

'How are you?' (*San ban oh?*)
'What time is it?' (*Tsag khed bolj baigan?*)
'No problem' (*Zugeer.*)

71

MOROCCO

Morocco. The sights, the sounds, the smells. Well, that's foreign food for you. But nevertheless, the atmosphere of a bustling Moroccan marketplace is familiar to us all. The haggling stallholders, the stalls piled high with spices, the exquisitely detailed carpets and fabrics, the wide range of cheap watchstraps and DVDs.

Greeting someone in the Moroccan marketplace is a highly involved process. You cannot get away with just calling, 'Wotcher, mate!', shouting, 'Oi wanker!' or simply chucking an aubergine at someone's head.

Saying hello to a Moroccan can last up to ten minutes and will involve a very warm form of greeting. You should shake hands with your right hand while exchanging pleasantries about friends, family and work. Occasionally throw in a touch to your chest to indicate how deeply moving you are finding the whole experience.

After ten minutes of this, you will be left feeling invigorated, thinking what lovely people the Moroccans are, and then following a glance at your watch you will realise you have just missed the last bus back to your hotel.

A Moroccan will therefore be really pleased to see you. So no, that isn't some sort of large gourd under their kaftan.

¡DON'T FORGET!

Morocco is a largely Muslim country and it is appropriate to dress modestly. Highly revealing bikinis should not be worn. Particularly if you are a man.

PHRASES TO REMEMBER

'Hello.' (*Salem Alekoum.*)
'How are your friends, family and work?'
    (*Kifash familia, soohab ou khadema diyelak.*)
'I have never seen such a large gourd before.'
    (*Oumari shouft shi khiar kbir kad hadi.*)

73

NEPAL

✪ Don't step over anyone's outstretched legs ✪

It is never a good idea to step over people. Not only is it impolite, you are also unlikely to get away with it because you will be traced by the footprints you leave on them. Despite this, in the West, people regularly walk over each other either out of impatience or to escape a disaster or to get their hands on a fantastic bargain in the January sales.

In Nepal, stepping over another person is completely taboo. If you sit with your legs, feet or any other part of your body stretched out across a doorway or thoroughfare, a Nepalese person will stand waiting until you move to let them pass. At no point will a Nepalese person decide to hop, skip or jump over you to get past.

So pull in your legs if a Nepalese person wishes to pass, avoid stepping over anyone in your rush to get up the Himalayas and never try to persuade any Nepalese to form a human pyramid with you.

Besides, Nepal is a very mountainous kingdom. Not stepping over someone's legs may be very practical. If you trip over a Sherpa halfway up Mount Everest, you could fall a long way down.

¡DON'T FORGET!

The Yeti or Abominable Snowman has never been found but footprints suggest the creature may have particularly enormous feet. Therefore, do not try stepping over a Yeti either.

> ### PHRASES TO REMEMBER
>
> 'Hello.' (*Namasté.*)
> 'What is this?' (*Yo ke ho?*)
> 'Do you love me?' (*Ke timi malai maya garchau?*)

NEW ZEALAND

✪ Be careful where you sit when you're Down Under ✪

Chairs, stools, benches and sofas. These are the items of furniture whose entire purpose in life is to provide resting places for human buttocks. These days, however, people also perch themselves on tables, desks, kitchen units and window ledges with varying degrees of success.

In New Zealand, plonking your behind on a table or desk is likely to offend. This is not just for the obvious reasons (e.g. sitting on something that someone was trying to read, sitting in someone's dinner or on someone's computer keyboard and accidentally pressing ctrl alt delete by breaking wind).

More seriously, the act of sitting on a table or desk is an ancient Maori taboo. The table where food is served or prepared should not be sullied by the unclean lower regions. As well as hygiene, the taboo may be associated with putting your body in the place of food and thus not treating yourself appropriately.

In recent years, offence has been caused in New Zealand by the broadcast of imported TV cookery shows in which presenters have been seen casually leaning against kitchen surfaces.

And quite right too! Arses should not be in our food! Or, indeed, presenting cookery programmes on TV!

¡DON'T FORGET!

New Zealanders particularly dislike being mistaken for Australians. So if you meet a New Zealander do not make the mistake of immediately trying to order a round of drinks from him.

> ### PHRASES TO REMEMBER
>
> 'Hello.' (*Hey.*)
> 'Do you like Jamie Oliver?' (*You better like Jamie Oliver!*)
> 'A pint of Foster's, please.' (*A pint of nasty piss, please.*)

NIGERIA

✪ A wink's as good as a nod ✪

A wink can mean many things. It can be a cheeky but friendly gesture or a surreptitious expression of understanding or a signal denoting sexual attraction or it can mean that you have something wrong with your eye.

In Nigeria, winking at children informs them that they should leave the room. If you are faced with a room of Nigerian children and cheerily wink at them one by one, you will see (with your remaining open eye) the room gradually empty before you.

At this point you may feel worried. Did you wink at the children in a manner that could have been deemed threatening or inappropriate? Are the children going to return in the company of a Nigerian police officer to whom they will solemnly point you out? What exactly are conditions like in Nigerian prisons?

You should therefore wink carefully when in a room with Nigerian children. Also, if you suffer from any sort of chronic facial tic you may find it tricky to gain employment as a schoolteacher in Lagos.

It would clearly be difficult for you to maintain discipline if every time you addressed your class, they left the room and assembled in the road outside.

¡DON'T FORGET!

The lottery is very popular in Nigeria, with people around the world regularly discovering they have won large cash prizes despite never having heard of the competition.

PHRASES TO REMEMBER

*'Hello.' (*Hi there.*)
'I have got something in my eye.' (*I'm not winking at you, I swear.*)
'Please come back into the classroom!' (*This looks worse than it is!*)
*English is the official language of Nigeria.

PAKISTAN

✪ Biting your thumbnails is a *really* bad habit ✪

And so we proceed around the globe offending yet more races and cultures using nothing more than our hands.

Welcome to Pakistan! Now make a fist, stick out your thumb and then flick the thumbnail against your front teeth. Doing this will upset people not only from Pakistan but from India as well. So in this at least the two nations are united.

And don't forget, both countries possess nuclear weapons, so upset them at your peril! OK, no country has so far carried out a nuclear strike in retaliation for someone making a rude gesture, but there's got to be a first time for everything.

You might think that biting your thumb is unlikely to hurt anyone except yourself but it will be taken as a terrible insult throughout the Indian subcontinent. If you perform this gesture in front of a Pakistani gentleman, you will be telling him to go and perform sexual services upon himself.

So avoid flicking your thumb off your teeth. The gesture is not only disgusting, it may also cause your front teeth to become dislodged and to be fired out of your mouth. At least that would stop you doing it again.

¡DON'T FORGET!

Urdu is the official language of Pakistan. It is not something you ask for in a Liverpool hairdressers.

PHRASES TO REMEMBER

'Hello.' (*Assalam-o-Alaikum.*)
'Nice to meet you.' (*Aap Se Milker Khushi Hui.*)
'Where do you live?' (*Aap Kahan Rahte Hain?*)

PAPUA NEW GUINEA

✪ Never step over food ✪

Papua New Guinea is famous for having over 850 indigenous languages. This could cause havoc if their road signs follow the method used in Wales of showing information in every language spoken locally.

Visitors to Papua New Guinea should be careful when shopping in the local marketplace to never step across any food laid out on the ground. If you do so, the food will be deemed unclean and inedible. This might seem a bit of an insult to your personal hygiene, but it is normal practice in the country.

The food that has been stepped over will thus be rendered worthless. Worthless, that is, to everyone except you, who will be expected to shell out a high price to pay for the goods. This will teach you not to sully Papuan produce in future and will provide compensation to the greengrocer in question.

This taboo particularly applies to women and particularly to women at certain times of the month. All in all, it's probably better to keep to the path around the market stalls and avoid leaping over the fruit and veg. And if you step over someone's child the situation is likely to deteriorate even further.

¡DON'T FORGET!

Headhunting was once widely practised in Papua New Guinea. This does not mean that if you wander into the forest you are likely to bump into a tribesperson who will help you find a high-powered executive job in the City.

> ### PHRASES TO REMEMBER
>
> *'Hello.' (*I have no idea which language to address you in.*)
> 'These vegetables taste like someone has stepped over them.'
>   (*I don't mind, but you seem to have a problem with it.*)
> 'What are you doing to my head?' (*That's beginning to hurt.*)
> *English is the official language of Papua New Guinea, but not the most popular.*

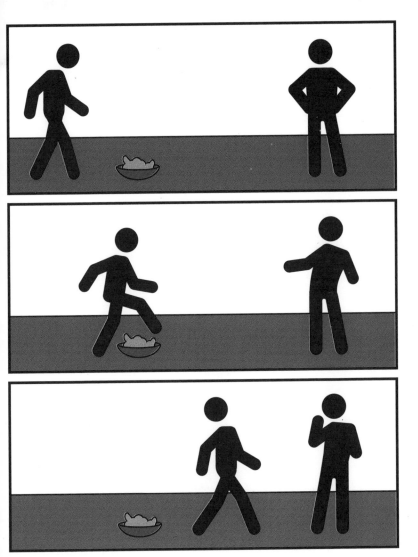

PHILIPPINES

✪ Here, boy! ✪

The Philippines, or the Phils to their friends, is an archipelago of 7,107 islands. It would be possible to use them as a set of stepping stones between Taiwan and Borneo (if you had a particularly long stride). The country was once famous for being the home of the Imelda Marcos shoe collection, but this has now had to be cleared away to make room for a rapidly increasing population.

If you want to upset a Filipino, try beckoning him towards you using a curling motion of the index finger. You know the one. The 'come hither into my boudoir' gesture, a.k.a. the 'come here, you!' index finger twitch beloved of Western school teachers.

In the Philippines, this gesture is very insulting as it is only used for dogs. You will therefore make the situation a lot worse if, after calling a Filipino over, you pop a choccy drop into his mouth.

You can therefore easily find yourself in a Philippine altercation. During the course of this, you may even get the offending finger broken, which should stop you doing it again. Unless of course you want to get through your remaining fingers by committing another seven similar offences.

¡DON'T FORGET!

The capital of the Philippines is Manila, which covers an area of 38.55 square kilometres and is the most densely populated city in the world. Hence the well-known expression, 'Manila envelops you'.

> ### PHRASES TO REMEMBER
>
> 'Hello.' (*Kumusta hô.*)
> 'Wait a minute.' (*Sandali lang.*)
> 'It doesn't matter.' (*Di bale.*)

POLAND

✪ Flick your neck ... and it's your round ✪

Poland – the large country in northern Europe famous for potatoes, beetroot, cabbage and being invaded by its neighbours. Poland gave the world Frederic Chopin, Pope John Paul II and Lech Walesa. It would have given more but these were the only Polish people whose names could be pronounced by non-Poles.

One good thing about Poland is that every word in its language will score you 50 points in Scrabble. Also, if you live in Poland you will probably never be short of a plumber.

Poles like to celebrate their names rather than their birthdays and different days of the year are allocated to different names. So if, for example, your name is Boguslaw you celebrate on 20 March with all the other Polish people called Boguslaw and may receive a Happy Boguslaw Day card.

Another Polish oddity is the gesture of flicking your neck. This is not considered rude but instead is an invitation from one male to another to join him for a drink.

So, if you spend too long scratching at your neck while on a visit to Poland, you may find a number of locals gathered around you and expecting to be bought a drink.

¡DON'T FORGET!

Despite the similarity in spelling to the word 'polish', rubbing Polish people on your furniture will not make the wood shine and could lead to a breakdown in international relations.

PHRASES TO REMEMBER

'Hello.' (*Cześć.*)
'Will you marry me?' (*Wyjdziesz za mnie?*)
'Please speak more slowly.' (*Prosze mówię wolniej.*)

PORTUGAL

✪ Asking for seasoning insults your chef ✪

We all know salt can be bad for you and in Portugal it is doubly so – particularly when it is brought to your table by a red-faced chef intent on shoving the saltcellar up your nose.

If you are dining out in Portugal and salt and pepper have not been set out on your table, do not call the waiter over to ask for them. Asking for additional seasoning or condiments will be taken as an insult as it casts aspersions on the skills of the chef who prepared your meal.

Never mind that you never eat a meal at home that isn't covered in enough salt to grit the entire Arctic ice shelf. Never mind that you are known to friends and family as 'a man for all seasonings'. Hold off with the salt or Portugal's answer to Gordon Ramsay will provide you with the Portuguese translation of Ramsay's colourful language.

So when in a Portuguese restaurant try to refrain from calling out, 'Could I have some salt and pepper and mustard and vinegar and tomato ketchup and mayonnaise and brown sauce and fruit sauce and mint sauce … and anything else you've got back there.'

¡DON'T FORGET!

Portuguese explorers include Bartholomew Dias, who was the first to sail round the southern tip of Africa, Vasco da Gama, who discovered the route to India, and Ferdinand Magellan, whose expedition was the first to sail right round the world. So when in Portugal avoid asking why so many of the inhabitants seem keen to get as far away from the country as possible.

PHRASES TO REMEMBER

'Hello.' (*Bom dia.*)
'Please, could I have some salt.'
(*Por favor, eu poderia ter um pouco de sal?*)
'Are there any famous Portuguese people who didn't leave the country?'
(*Existem algumas pessoas famosas Português que não deixar o país?*)

RUSSIA

✪ Shaking hands across a threshold is unlucky ✪

A shake of the hand is a friendly gesture. There are occasions, however, when it is a bad idea, for instance if the two people concerned are in separate vehicles travelling in opposite directions or if one of them is connected to a high-voltage power supply.

In Russia, it is considered unlucky to shake hands across a threshold or doorway. According to local tradition, joining hands across a doorway creates a bridge which can be used by evil spirits to enter a building.

So if you want to shake hands with a Russian, get them to come out into the hallway to you. Then a few moments later you can help them get back into their flat after their door accidentally closes and locks behind them.

As well as not shaking hands, Russians also don't like to hand over items across a threshold. So yes, this cultural taboo genuinely makes life difficult for Russian pizza-delivery people.

You should also never shake hands across the entrance to a lift. This is for more practical reasons as the lift doors may suddenly close leaving the trapped hand pathetically waving for help as it is dragged upwards to the ceiling.

¡DON'T FORGET!

Russia is the biggest country in the world by area. You could fit 70 countries the size of the UK into it, although attempting to do this in reality could be difficult and time consuming.

PHRASES TO REMEMBER

'Hello.' (*Zdravstvujte.*)
'Leave me alone!' (*Ostav'te menja v pokoe!*)
'This gentleman will pay for everything.' (*Etot mužčina platit za vsë*)

SAMOA

✪ No seats? Just use someone's lap ✪

In past times, few tourists reached the remote Pacific island of Samoa. In fact, it used to be regularly reported that only 'one man went to Samoa', although this individual did seem to keep returning with his dog and a growing number of friends.

These days, Samoa is much more on the tourist trail. If, however, you travel by bus on the island, you should be prepared for unusual seating arrangements.

Climbing onto a crowded bus or underground train and having to stand pressed up against a mass of strangers is never pleasant. Fortunately, in Samoa, you never have to stand with your fellow passengers. You get to sit on them instead.

Standing is not permitted on Samoan buses. If your bus arrives packed full of passengers, the solution favoured by many Samoans is to get on and sit on the lap of one of the other passengers. Well, they are a famously friendly people.

So, if you're on a crowded bus in Samoa and someone asks, 'Is anyone sitting there?' while pointing at your lap, it may be time to brace yourself.

¡DON'T FORGET!

Samoa gave the world the concept and word 'tattoo'. The islands of Samoa only cover just over 1,000 square miles. If the total area of human flesh now covered by tattoos is included as Samoan territory, the country now covers an area similar to the size of Russia.

PHRASES TO REMEMBER

'Hello.' (*Talofa.*)
'Pleased to meet you.' (*Fiafia ua ta feiloai.*)
'How was your day?' (*O fa'apefea mai lou aso?*)

SAUDI ARABIA

✪ The left hand is the dirty hand ✪

Saudi Arabia is not short of cultural taboos for the unwary Western traveller. In fact, it's something of a Mecca for them. One practice that is found not only in Saudi Arabia but in other Arab countries, parts of Africa, the Indian subcontinent and through to Southeast Asia is that relating to use of the left hand.

Arabs will be offended if you use your left hand to greet them, to pass anything to them or to handle food. This is because the left hand is regarded as the unclean hand. It is the hand reserved for personal hygiene.

It's the bottom-wiping hand, OK!

So are people from Morocco to Vietnam really using their left hands to wipe their backsides, with maybe only a bowl of water to assist in the process and not a sheet of Andrex in sight? No, of course not. The earliest evidence for the production of soap was almost 5,000 years ago in Babylon (85 km south of Baghdad). So Arabs have had lovely clean hands for several thousand years.

Nevertheless, there remains a strong cultural stigma against the left hand. So when visiting Arab friends remember not to wipe yours on the curtains.

¡DON'T FORGET!

Although 95 per cent of Saudi Arabia is sand, this does not mean that if there is a sudden gust of wind most of the country will disappear.

PHRASES TO REMEMBER

'Hello.' (*Salem Alekoum.*)
'Yes, we have toilet paper.' (*Eyeah, kain al warkha d'iel kanif.*)
'Your left hand smells funny.' (*Y'edik anda nsmah fshkil*)

SENEGAL

✪ Don't be a crybaby ✪

These days people cry all the time. TV talent shows regularly feature contestants crying, footballers cry after a penalty is missed, celebrity interviews are never complete without the subject blubbing at some point and, as many young men know, crying is the ultimate desperate method that can be used to persuade someone to sleep with you.

Crying is, however, less popular in the West African country of Senegal. Senegalese people are taught not to show emotion under any circumstance. They resemble the staff in Top Shop in this respect. Senegalese women in particular are raised to stifle any indication of their feelings, while crying is regarded as a sign of weakness.

So, if you visit Senegal, avoid breaking out in tears at all cost. Never mind that you have stubbed your toe, your football team has just been relegated or you can't get a mobile signal.

It is not that the good people will ridicule you for your display of emotion. No, instead they will be alarmed and terrified by the sight. Crying to them indicates that the most terrible disaster imaginable must have just occurred.

So, pull yourself together, wipe away your tears and stop causing chaos in Senegal!

¡DON'T FORGET!

The national language of Senegal is French, but this should not confuse visitors into thinking that they are in France. Hence the name of the country, which is clearly an abbreviation of the phrase 'Ce n'est pas Gaul'. (This joke is one of the few things that is actually capable of making a Senegalese person cry.)

PHRASES TO REMEMBER

'Hello.' (*Bonjour.*)
'Have you got a handkerchief?' (*Est-ce que vous avez un mouchoir?*)
'Do not panic. I am just peeling an onion.' (*Ne panic pas. Je suis juste entrain d'éplucher un oignon.*)

SINGAPORE

✪ Fined for not flushing ✪

Singapore is one of the smallest countries in the world. And with around 6,430 people per square kilometre it is also in the world's top three most densely populated countries. And with that many people living in that small a space, no wonder Singapore has some stringent regulations to make its residents behave themselves while on the toilet.

If you visit Singapore and fail to flush the toilet after using it, you could end up in deep doo-doo. The Singapore authorities have in recent years introduced a fine of $75 for those who fail to turn the handle or pull the chain.

Admittedly, you would be quite unlucky to open your cubicle door and find an elite team from the Singapore toilet squad standing outside waiting for you.

On the other hand, this is not a crime for which anyone would enjoy being named and shamed. When the local equivalent of *Crimewatch* comes on the TV, you don't want a CCTV image of yourself sitting with your pants round your ankles to appear in between pictures of Singapore's most wanted criminals.

¡DON'T FORGET!

It is also against the law in Singapore to urinate in a lift. Presumably, however, this is not so unusual a law. There are few countries where weeing in elevators is socially and legally acceptable. Besides, if the lift is crowded, other people are bound to notice what you're up to.

PHRASES TO REMEMBER

'Hello.' (*Ni hao.*)
'I don't understand.' (*Wo ting bù dong.*)
'Thank you.' (*Xiè xiè.*)

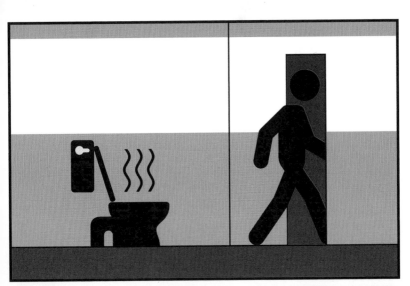

SOUTH AFRICA

✪ The 'fist fig' gesture is obscene ✪

South Africa – its name is quite handy if you're unsure where to find it. It's located in the most southern part of Africa.

South Africa is one of a number of countries where the fig gesture is considered insulting, obscene and disgusting. Other countries are unaware that the gesture exists at all or that there is anything that rude about figs.

In order to make the fig gesture, clench your fist. Then stick the end of your thumb out between your first and second fingers. Now show this to a South African. If they start quivering with anger, congratulations! You have made 'the fig'! Now prepare to get beaten up!

Use of the fig gesture will disgust and appal a range of nationalities. In Italy it is known as 'far la fica', in France 'faire la figue' and in Spain 'hacer el higo'. The gesture is believed to be upsetting in these cultures because of the fist being made to resemble the appearance of the female genitals. Just think of the fun young boys must be able to have in these countries simply by having a crafty look at their own fists.

¡DON'T FORGET!

The popular trick of stealing someone's nose and then showing it back to them between your fingers involves an identical use of the end of the thumb poked through the first and second fingers. It is therefore a very bad idea to play this game with a small child in South Africa, Italy, France or Spain, particularly if their parents are nearby.

PHRASES TO REMEMBER!

'Hello.' (*Howsit, yah.*)
'Would you like a fig?' (*Wanna fig, yah?*)
'Look, I have stolen your nose.' (*Got your nose, yah.*)

SOUTH KOREA

✪ Number 4 – unlucky for some ✪

South Korea – home to electronics companies Samsung and LG and also to the world's most dangerous golf course (it's on the border with North Korea, consists of only one hole but is surrounded on three sides by minefields – which should help improve the accuracy of your drive).

But even a golf course with an exploding sand trap is nothing to Koreans compared to the number 4! In Korea, the number 4 is considered to be extremely unlucky. The number has such bad associations that it is not listed on the control panels of Korean lifts and is referred to instead by the letter 'F'.

Korea is not the only country in the world to require euphemistic lift controls. Number 4 is also considered unlucky in China and Japan as in these countries' languages it sounds similar to the word for death. And getting into a lift in which the options are floors 1, 2, 3 or death would surely worry anyone.

And because the number 4 is so unlucky, Koreans believe gifts should never be given in multiples of 4. The number 7, on the other hand, is considered to be lucky. Well, it's 3 more gifts for a start!

¡DON'T FORGET!

North Korea is the communist state ruled by the Dear Leader Kim Jong Il. If you find yourself surrounded by lots of people in uniform marching in step while balancing a nuclear warhead on their shoulders, you have wandered into the wrong Korea.

PHRASES TO REMEMBER

'How do you do?' (*Ch'oum poepgetsumnida?*)
'Would you like to go out with me?' (*Narang sagwillaeyo?*)
'We split up.' (*Uri heeojyeosseo.*)

SPAIN

✪ Not rude to stare ✪

Most people feel uncomfortable if someone fixes them with a long hard stare. Even dogs react badly if you stare at them.

In Spain and parts of South America, however, local people have clearly never been told it is rude to stare. Instead, they may fix you with a sultry, lingering look. Oddly enough, Spanish men may particularly stare at attractive young women. If they are staring at you even though you are an unattractive older man, check your flies aren't undone.

Women travellers are told that this hot-blooded Latin staring should not be taken as offensive. Instead, it should be regarded as a compliment! As compliments go, it may be one of the more intimidating ones to receive.

So don't worry if Spanish men stare at you. Maybe they are doing it because it's so hot in Spain they don't have the energy to move their heads very much. Maybe there isn't anything worth watching on Spanish television. Maybe they are just building up to a sudden frenzied burst of flamenco dancing.

Or maybe they are doing it until you begin to feel self-conscious and do something stupid like losing your balance and falling over in front of them.

¡DON'T FORGET!

The rain in Spain falls mainly on the plain. So, if you don't want to get wet, always go out wearing some sort of exotic or colourful costume.

PHRASES TO REMEMBER

'Hello.' (*¡Hola!*)
'Why are you staring at me?' '(*¿Por qué me estás mirando fijamente?*)
'My dog just bit you because you were staring at it.'
    (*Mi perro te ha mordido porque le miraba fijo.*)

SWITZERLAND

✪ Dropping litter is heavily frowned upon ✪

The Swiss have never bothered joining the European Union and if there's any trouble between the neighbours, such as World War I or II, they keep well out of it.

Instead, they like to sit eating chocolate, watching their cuckoo clocks and counting the vast amounts of other people's money left in their keeping. It is even said to be illegal in Switzerland to flush the toilet after 10 p.m. or to mow the lawn on Sunday. Well, you know what kind of anarchy follows if you allow that sort of thing.

Furthermore, the Swiss are keen to keep their country nice and tidy. Their roads and pavements are all kept spotless. For all we know, the Swiss regularly go out with vacuum cleaners to clean the streets. Obviously they don't do this on Sunday because that would be illegal.

So if you want to upset the Swiss just drop a few bits of litter and see how long they stay neutral then. This might be what it finally takes to get the Swiss Army out in force.

Although you'd better watch out in case the Swiss Army come after you with all those attachments they have on their knives.

¡DON'T FORGET!

Many ancient tribes of northern Europe such as the Goths and the Vandals are remembered for being violent and warlike. The ancient inhabitants of Switzerland, by contrast, are remembered today because the Helvetica font was named after them.

PHRASES TO REMEMBER

*'Hello.' (*Bonjour.*)
'Could you pick your litter up, please.'
(*Ramasser votre poubelle s'il vous plaît.*)
'Switch off that lawn mower. It is Sunday.'
(*Éteigniez votre tondeuse à gazon. C'est dimanche.*)
*Switzerland has four official languages: French, German, Italian & Romansh. French will do.

TAIWAN

✪ Don't cuddle that chair ✪

Taiwan should not be confused with China. This is difficult, as Taiwan is quite near China and is formally known as the Republic of China. China itself is the slightly less official-sounding People's Republic of China. The Taiwanese also have a range of Chinese taboos such as those relating to physical contact.

Around the rest of the world, finding another person's hand down your back will provoke different reactions depending on circumstances such as your relationship to the person concerned, how cold their hand is and whether or not you are a ventriloquist's dummy.

In Taiwan, however, you should never place your arm across someone's back. You should not even place your arm across the back of a chair in which someone is sitting. This level of overfamiliarity is considered offensive and taboo. If you want to get amorous with someone's chair, wait until the person has stood up and walked away.

It is similarly inappropriate to give a Taiwanese person a friendly pat on the back or shoulders. Nor should you pat anyone on the head.

In fact, generally just avoid performing any impromptu massage on any casual acquaintances you make in Taiwan.

¡DON'T FORGET!

Competition seems to exist between the Republic of China and the People's Republic of China as regards which of them is really China. This doesn't happen with other countries. You don't, for example, get rivalry between the South Sandwich Islands and the People's South Sandwich Islands.

PHRASES TO REMEMBER

'Hello.' (*Ni hao.*)
'I don't understand.' (*Wo fingbudong.*)
'Do you understand?' (*Dong ma?*)

THAILAND

✪ It is disrespectful to tread on the king ✪

The residents of Thailand have a deep reverence for their monarch Bhumibol Adulyadej, Rama IX, the Great that goes beyond the regard for the Queen that is felt in the UK. Even by readers of the *Daily Mail*.

Thais carry the image of their king on talismans to bring them good luck. They love their king and will not appreciate any joke or satirical comment about him. So do not be tempted to make even the mildest witticism about the pronunciation of his first name.

And any act of defacing an image of the king will not just be poorly received it could also put you in prison. In 2007, a Swiss man was jailed for ten years for writing graffiti on a poster that bore an image of the king's face. He had only wanted to protest at not being allowed to buy alcohol on the king's birthday.

You should also never ever tread on a picture of the King of Thailand. This even applies to Thai coins which carry his image. So, if you drop a 10 baht coin and it starts rolling away from you, stopping it with your foot could land you in a Thai jail!

¡DON'T FORGET!

Until 1939, Thailand was known as Siam. This does not mean that Bangkok can only ever be twinned with other cities that are right next to it.

PHRASES TO REMEMBER

'Hello.' (*Sawa dee.*)
'Do you understand?' (*Kow jai mai.*)
'Nevermind.' (*Mai pen rai.*)

TIBET

○ Sticking your tongue out is polite ○

Don't take it the wrong way if a Tibetan sticks his tongue out at you. In Tibet, this gesture indicates modesty and respect for others. It is unlikely to be accompanied by the churning sound of approaching vomit unless, of course, your Tibetan friend has recently consumed some past-its-use-by-date yak's milk.

Apparently, the sticking-the-tongue-out custom derives from many centuries ago. When a Tibetan performs this action he is informing you that he is not the reincarnation of the ancient, horn-headed, black-tongued emperor, Langdarma. And this news will be of considerable relief.

Langdarma was the last emperor of the unified Tibetan empire and reigned from 838 to 841. Langdarma persecuted the Buddhists before being assassinated by a Buddhist monk. So far so good, but, as Buddhists believe in reincarnation, this means Langdarma may return at any time.

Showing off your tongue will therefore tell any passing Tibetans, 'See my pink tongue! I am not the reincarnation of Langdarma! Now you may relax!'

Beware, however, if you take a box of Liquorice Allsorts to eat during a walking tour of Tibet. After a few hours chomping, the blackened appearance of your tongue may cause widespread panic across the country.

¡DON'T FORGET!

Tibet is the size of Western Europe but slightly higher up. To be a little more precise, it is 2.65 miles (14,000 feet) above sea level. So, if you visit, be careful you don't fall off.

PHRASES TO REMEMBER

'Hello.' (*Tashi deleg.*)
'Do you speak English?' (*In-ji-ke shing-gi-yo-pe?*)
'Sorry.' (*Gonad.*)

TURKEY

✪ Don't blow your nose in public ✪

Turkey is the land where Asia meets Europe, East meets West, and Turkey meets eight other countries. Yes, Turkey has land borders with Greece, Bulgaria, Georgia, Armenia, Azerbaijan, Iran, Iraq and Syria. So, if you take a wrong turn while travelling through the country, you could be in for an exciting time.

Turkey shares many cultural taboos with Eastern countries. For example, in Turkey, there is an emphasis on hygiene and cleanliness. Well, they invented the Turkish bath. Turks are also often concerned about catching colds and flu. Surely anyone would be the same if they lived on a global crossroads. Who knows what bugs might be carried through each day?

One thing you should never do in public in Turkey is blow your nose. This is considered the height of bad manners. If you add any accompanying trumpeting noises, this will make the situation even worse. Should you get the sniffles in Turkey, you should excuse yourself, retire to another room – or possibly pop across the border into a different country – before filling your hanky full of Eastern promise.

And no, it's not because they're worried about bird flu that the country is called Turkey.

¡DON'T FORGET!

The inflation rate is very high in Turkey and prices even for just a small item may be in the millions of lira (although the New Turkish lira was introduced in 2005 which dropped six zeros from the end of the old lira). So, if you win the top prize on the Turkish version of *Who Wants To Be A Millionaire*, you may only have won enough to buy a bottle of Coca-Cola.

PHRASES TO REMEMBER!

'Hello.' (*Merhaba.*)
'Are you married?' (*Evli misiniz?*)
'I'm drunk!' (*Sarhoš oldum!*)

UGANDA

✪ It's normal for two men to hold hands ✪

In Uganda, public displays of affection are considered offensive. This will be the case even if neither you nor your partner is old or ugly.

In Uganda, you will, however, often see two men walking along holding hands. This is neither a public display of affection nor a sign that one of the men is trying to steal a wristwatch from the other. It is merely a sign that they are good friends.

In Western countries such as Britain, men only hold hands in extreme circumstances, for example if one of them is extraordinarily drunk and needs to be guided away from falling to his death off a high roof. Even then, the drunk man's friend may be unable to bring himself to hold hands.

Clearly, there should be more inter-male hand holding in Western society. How wonderful it would be to see British men with their hairy little hands entwined as they walk to the pub, to a football match or just along to work at the docks.

For a start, it would save a lot of men from getting lost. They often have a poor sense of direction and famously refuse to ever ask for directions.

¡DON'T FORGET!

Countries in which men hold hands do not tend to be places in which homosexuality is openly tolerated. In fact, quite the opposite. You should therefore avoid skipping up to any hand-holding men squealing, 'Sisters! How marvellous to see you coming out like this!'

> ### PHRASES TO REMEMBER
> 'What's up?' (*Ki kati?*)
> 'I do not have any money.' (*Sirina Sente.*)
> 'What is that?' (*Ekyo kiki?*)

UKRAINE

☺ Even numbers of flowers are only given at funerals ☺

In Ukraine, a dozen red roses does not say 'I love you'. Instead, it says, 'Rest in peace, my darling. You are going to drop dead at any moment!'

Give a Ukrainian woman flowers and she will be delighted … but only if you have given her the correct number of blooms. Once your floral gift has been presented, your Ukrainian girlfriend will proceed to count them out. 'Ras, dva, tri, chotiri, pyat, sheest …' That's counting in Ukrainian. Obviously if you have given a large bouquet the process may take several minutes.

If it turns out that you have given an even number of flowers, the romantic mood may abruptly change. In Ukraine, even numbers of flowers are only taken to funerals and are otherwise considered extremely unlucky.

So if you give a Ukrainian lady an even number of flowers you are not telling her how much you admire her. Instead, you are reminding her of her own death. And that's never a good idea on a first date.

Your Ukrainian lady friend may then say something with flowers back to you by stuffing your gift somewhere that doesn't involve a vase.

¡DON'T FORGET!

Ukraine has given the world many things but the main one that everyone remembers is the nuclear cloud that emanated from the Chernobyl region in April 1986.

PHRASES TO REMEMBER

'Hello.' (*Doh-brihy dehn.*)
'What's new?' (*Shcho novogo?*)
'Ukraine is a beautiful country.' (Ukraina – krasïva kraïna)

UAE

✪ No canoodling in public ✪

The United Arab Emirates is an exciting modern-looking country studded with gleaming new shops and offices. Nevertheless, it is also a Muslim nation with strict codes of behaviour.

Sex between unmarried couples is officially illegal, skimpy clothing is unacceptable and swearing and obscene gestures will get you into trouble. If these rules were applied in Britain, some entire town centres could be closed down.

Public displays of affection should also be avoided, no matter how irresistible your partner may be. In Dubai in 2010, a British couple were jailed for a month for kissing in a public place. That's not a euphemism, by the way. They were in a restaurant. Also, for good measure, a fine was slapped on them because they were drinking alcohol.

Two years earlier, a British man and woman were threatened with six years in prison for having sex on a Dubai beach. That counts as another unacceptable public display of affection. Again, you should avoid repeating this sort of thing in the UAE, especially in restaurants in front of other diners. In the end, the couple involved were given three-month jail sentences.

So having sex in public is officially only three times worse than kissing!

¡DON'T FORGET!

Possession of drugs will mean serious consequences in the UAE. Even just having a few poppy seeds hidden about your person could get you into trouble. So, if you've recently eaten a seeded bread roll, make sure you give your teeth a good flossing before arriving in Dubai.

PHRASES TO REMEMBER

'Hello.' (*Salem Alekoum.*)
'I would like to kiss you in a private place.'
    (*Khasni boussek fe shi mota m'khabara.*)
'A small seeded loaf, please.' (*A tini shi koubza srera ou zraa, afek.*)

UNITED KINGDOM

✪ Which way do the fingers go again, Winston? ✪

The 'V for victory' sign, a.k.a. the peace sign. You can't go wrong with that, can you? Well, you can in the UK.

Here, the two-fingered salute has slightly different tones of meaning depending on its orientation. With the palm facing outwards, it says, 'Peace and love to all the world, brothers and sisters!' With the back of the hand facing outwards, the same gesture says, 'Fuck off!'

Yes, it's these little nuances and subtleties that make British society so fascinating. They also help involve hundreds of visitors to the country in unexpected fights with locals following innocent attempts to order two pints of beer in a British pub or to inform someone that the time is two o'clock.

According to legend (i.e. someone made this story up), the meaning of the knuckles-forward V-sign dates back to the Battle of Agincourt in 1415. The French threatened that following their victory they would chop off the fingers of the English and Welsh archers leaving them unable to use their bows.

The French, of course, went on to lose the battle and 600 years later the British still never miss an opportunity to make the V-sign at them.

¡DON'T FORGET!

Even wartime Prime Minister Winston Churchill seemed confused about the V-sign. By the end of the war, he had learned to do the 'V for victory' sign with his knuckles inward but earlier he was regularly pictured making the 'fuck off' version. Or perhaps he was just telling the lower orders what he thought of them.

PHRASES TO REMEMBER

'Hello.' (*Fuck off!*)
'Two pints of beer please!' (*Fuck off!*)
'Do you want to see my Winston Churchill impression?' (*Fuck off!*)

USA

✪ Avoid giving the 'finger' ✪

Americans are friendly people who enjoy visiting countries all over the world either in the form of a holiday or a military invasion. And so the Yanks have helped spread the global popularity of the single-finger salute. Yes, the USA is indeed the country that gave the 'finger' to the world.

The 'finger', also known as 'flipping the bird', can be performed by inverting the hand with the middle finger raised and pointing upwards. The gesture conveys the meanings 'Screw yourself on this', 'Up yours' and/or 'Fuck you', if not all three jolly expressions combined in a single concise flick of the wrist. So don't try using this gesture to endear yourself to an American.

The 'digitus impudicus' dates back at least to Ancient Rome, when the historian Suetonius described how the entertainer Pylades was expelled by Augustus after making 'an obscene movement of his middle finger'.

As it requires only a single raised finger, 'the bird' is one of the least strenuous obscene gestures to perform. This is useful if you have never eaten anything except Happy Meals so you now weigh 300 pounds and cannot raise any other part of your body without the use of a hoist.

¡DON'T FORGET!

If you are pulled over by the police while driving in the United States, wait in your vehicle until the officer comes to you. Do not leap out of your vehicle and trot over to say 'hi' or this will be interpreted as meaning, 'Hello! I would like to volunteer to be used for target practice with immediate effect!'

PHRASES TO REMEMBER

'Hello.' (*Howdy, pardner!*)
'I think I have got something wrong with my middle finger.'
   (*My digitus impudicus is doggone sore.*)
'Please put your gun down.'
   (*Don't panic none, mister. I ain't packin' no heat.*)

VIETNAM

○ Bad things come in threes ○

When travelling through foreign lands, you may occasionally wish to take a photograph of one of the local people. You may be attracted by their colourful native dress, by the character etched in their features or simply by the extraordinary size and shape of their nose.

It is, however, polite to ask before taking such a picture and you should immediately desist if your subject seems unwilling to participate. Nothing spoils a slideshow of your holiday snaps more than a series of images of angry-looking foreign people having their photos taken against their will.

If you wish to photograph yourself standing with a travelling companion and a Vietnamese person, the Vietnamese person may be particularly reluctant. This is because a superstition exists that it is unlucky for three people to be photographed together. It is mainly unlucky for the person standing in the middle of the group as they will die soon afterwards.

So stand in the middle of the group yourself. Your Vietnamese friend will then be happy to pose with you, safe in the knowledge that you will be the one who will shortly meet your end (possibly leaving an expensive digital camera behind for him in the process).

¡DON'T FORGET!

The Vietnamese currency is called the dong. If a Vietnamese mugger holds you up and tells you to hand over your dong, do not get confused.

PHRASES TO REMEMBER

'Hello.' (*Xin chao.*)
'Can you help me?' (*Ban giup toi duoc khong?*)
'I'll be right back.' (*Tôi sẽ quay lải ngay*)

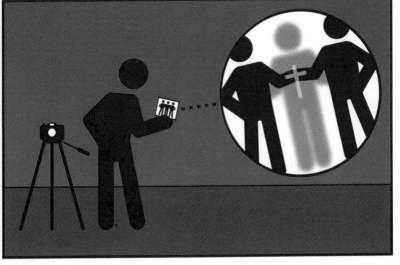

THANKS TO THE EXCELLENT MALCOLM CROFT, WILLIE RYAN AND CLAIRE MARSHALL, MY LONG SUFFERING FAMILY AND EVERYONE ELSE IN THE WORLD – PARTICULARLY THOSE WITH SLIGHTLY UNUSUAL CUSTOMS.